Listen, Little Dog!

igloo

Little Sheep Dog was very proud of his dad, who had just won a blue ribbon for being a champion sheep dog.
"One day, I'm going to win a blue ribbon just like you!" said Little Sheep Dog.

"To be a top sheep dog," said his dad, "you need to be able to move quickly and listen very carefully to what you are told."

But Little Sheep Dog was not listening. He was watching his friends running towards a big oak tree.

"We've found a beehive," shouted Little Sheep Dog's friends.
"Wait for me!" he said excitedly. "I've never seen one before."
"Be careful, Little Sheep Dog," called out his dad.
But Little Sheep Dog was not listening.

At the oak tree, Little Sheep Dog looked up at the beehive.
"I'm going to see if there is any honey inside," he said.
"Watch out for the bees, Little Sheep Dog!" called out his friends.

But Little Sheep Dog was not listening.
As he put his paw into the beehive,
a loud buzzing sound filled the air

BUZZZZZZZZZZZZ!

"You can't catch me, bees!" laughed Little Sheep Dog, "Sheepdogs are too fast."
"Watch where you're going, Little Sheep Dog!" warned his friends.

But Little Sheep Dog was not listening.
SPLASH! He landed right in the middle of a muddy pond.

"BRRR! The water is f-f-freezing!," shivered Little Sheep Dog.
"I had better shake myself dry before I catch a cold."
"Stop, Little Sheep Dog!" cried out his friends,
"or you will get us all wet!"

But Little Dog was not listening. As he shook and shook and shook, he covered his friends and Ram in water.

"Look at Ram," laughed Little Sheep Dog, "He's soaking wet!"
"I wouldn't be wet if you had listened," bleated Ram.

Ram chased Little Sheep Dog out of the pond, down the lane, through the gate and across the farmyard straight into a...

...slimy, stinky pile of squelchy muck!

"Are you alright?" asked Little Sheep Dog's friends.
"No! I'm not!" he whimpered. "I'm fed up, tired and — sniff — very smelly!"

That evening Little Sheep Dog settled down
for sleep with his dad.
"I'll never be a good sheep dog," he sighed
unhappily. "I always seem to end up in trouble."

"You just need to listen, Little Sheep Dog," said his dad, softly. "Then you will know what to do next."
"All I can hear right now is snoring animals," yawned Little Sheep Dog, as he drifted off to sleep.

In the middle of the night, Little Sheep Dog suddenly woke up.
"Baa! Baa!"
"That sounds like Ram," thought Little Sheep Dog. He got
up and crept quickly out of the barn, just in time to
see a dark shape slinking towards the sheep — a fox!

Little Sheep Dog bounded towards the fox, barking as loudly as he could.
"Get away from my sheep," he barked as the frightened fox ran back across the hill.

"I'm so glad you heard my bleats for help, Little Sheep Dog," smiled Ram the next day. The farm animals all agreed that Little Sheep Dog deserved a very special reward for being so brave.